D1526145

Threads of Grace

A story of Adoption, Reunion and Renewal

Mary Roberts

WESTBOW
PRESS®
A DIVISION OF THOMAS NELSON
& ZONDERVAN

WestBow Press books may be ordered through booksellers or by contacting:

WestBow Press
A Division of Thomas Nelson & Zondervan
1663 Liberty Drive
Bloomington, IN 47403
www.westbowpress.com
844-714-3454

ISBN: 978-1-9736-7704-8 (sc)
ISBN: 978-1-9736-7705-5 (e)

Library of Congress Control Number: 2019915806

Print information available on the last page.

WestBow Press rev. date: 09/28/2020

Epilogue

"If I told you my story
You would hear Grace, that wouldn't let go
and if I told you my story
you would hear Love that never gave up
and if I told you my story
you would hear Life …
… to tell you my story is to tell of Him …"
Song lyrics, Big Daddy Weave
My Story

Acknowledgement Page

Two people who encouraged me and stood by me are the catalyst for the finished product. Foremost is my husband. He created a safe and inspiring place for me to write, but never gave up hope that one day the book would be finished. Next, a beautiful woman who continues to surprise me with her grace and willingness to help. Spending hours editing for and alongside me, making me smile, and sharing her insights. Your help is invaluable and your friendship eternal. Thank-you.

Chapter 1

My fist clinched the coins as I walked to the pay phone. Anxiety and fear made it difficult to concentrate. How do I tell her? How will mom respond to the discouraging news?

I placed the receiver back in the hook and stared at the phone. The certainty of my situation was clear. I was on my own and soon to be homeless. I felt abandoned and alone. I imagined starting fresh, but a desperate hopelessness consumed me. Agonizing thoughts stumbled over each other.

Born the older of two daughters, my mother grew up as an only child after her nine-year-old sister's drowning death. Our family pictures were kept in an album except one. The picture of a young girl with blue eyes and blonde hair.

"Mommy who is in that picture?"

"That is my sister"

"Where is she?"

"She died."

Satisfied with her answer Mary ran off to play. Ruth poured a cup of coffee and thought back to the day she lost her best friend.

Cross-legged on the floor, she watched his mouth form the words, but what he said did not make sense.

"It will just be the three of us now. Do you understand?"

"Daddy, when is Betsy coming home, can I go see her in the hospital? She was never coming home.

The child of an Evangelical pastor, Ruth was a model student and daughter. After graduation at seventeen, she looked forward to college. Bible college in Florida. Minnesota was a nice place to grow up in, but Ruth loved the beach and the way the sun warmed her skin.

A pretty college student, Ruth juggled homework and weekly dates. A common place to take a date was the beach. Within walking distance from school, it was a popular hangout. A deep desire to become a wife and mother, Ruth accepted most invitations.

Friday nights young marines played beach volleyball and watched the college girls. Placing her towel near the game that was in progress, Ruth saw him. One of his friends noticed her looking their direction.

"See that cute blonde over there, she's watching you man."

"Shut up and serve."

The game was over. Ruth was not ready to leave. Thinking she had been discreet as she watched him, he approached and introduced himself.

"Hello, my name is Charles, what's yours?"

He had sad eyes, but a warm smile. The attraction was overwhelming and soon they were an item.

Her second year of bible college and in love with a marine. Ruth never dreamed things would turn out this way. A reckless man, Charles was the product of a broken and dysfunctional childhood filled with much hate and hurt. Telling him no was impossible. Either his anger or charisma won out over any objection.

The white wedding dress she dreamed of was replaced with a powder blue one. Six months after a June wedding, Ruth gave birth to their first daughter, Mary.

Not long after Mary was born, they sent Charles's unit to Laos. The Vietnam conflict had not yet morphed into a full-on war, but there were long-lasting effects of the tour of duty experienced by the men of his regiment, and Charles was no exception. Two years as a marine ended with a dishonorable discharge for multiple counts of insubordination.

Her marriage to Charles was not the partnership she envisioned. Dwindling finances and a need for housing forced the couple to move. They settled in a nearby town, rented a small trailer and Charles found a job fixing cars. Married five years when the youngest, a boy, was born.

Mom to four young children was no easy task. Long hours at work and emotionally distant, Ruth could not count on Charles for much support. Adultery plagued their marriage from the beginning. The pain of betrayal was a burden Ruth never wanted to carry. Her faith in a God who knows best, helped keep her family together.

Chapter 2

Dressed in our Sunday best my siblings and I stood side by side for inspection. Uncharacteristically, mom had not said anything during the drive to church that night. Once the car was parked, she spoke,

"I want you all on your best behavior, do you understand?

"Yes ma'am" was our collective response.

Unlike most services, few seats were filled. Members sat on one side of the church sanctuary while the four of us, with our mother, sat alone on the other. Sideways glances and murmuring made me feel uncomfortable. Mom, her posture was impeccable until pastor started speaking. Her shoulders fell then her head. Focused on mom I did not see Charles or Miss Kathy sitting on the stage.

"Charles, please come to the podium."

Startled, I jerked my head toward the stage.

"You have heard the charges against you and the reasons for this gathering. Do you have anything to say?"

"No"

"I will ask you again. Will you repent of the sin of adultery?"

"No"

"Charles, you are excommunicated from this church and are never to return.

Mumbling, Charles walked out of church for the last time.

Hurriedly, mom herded us towards the door. We left church that evening to looks of pity and shock. My feelings about church changed that day. The youngest, only six, fell asleep on the drive home. Permission was given to go into the house once the car was parked. Racing to the door, I couldn't wait to get out of my clothes. By the time mom came into the house, our brother in her arms, we had changed and turned on the television.

Not Charles' first or last affair, the only one made public. The abuse, physical and sexual continued. We pretended our life was something it was not for fear of punishment.

Chapter 3

The oldest of four kids and expected to live a nearly flawless life, I fell short. Lovingly, mom encouraged us with kindness and taught us life skills. Dad worked hard to tear us down, find fault, and abuse. The earliest memories I have of Charles are of his explosive outbursts of anger. Loud swearing and unkind things he screamed at us when we misbehaved. Spankings which left welts the length of the back of our legs.

Television was limited to a few shows and Saturday morning cartoons. I tiptoed past our parents' bedroom cartoons on my mind. The sight of the birdcage on its side, our pet bird in the cat's mouth made me scream. Tears streamed down my face as I ran to mom's side of the bed and yelled for help. What happened next was unexpected and wretched.

Charles, not a person who responded well to being woken by the crying screams of a ten-year-old, stomped into the living room. When he saw what the cat had done, he clutched my cat holding it by its neck. Grabbing my hair with his other hand he kicked open the locked front door then loosened his grip on my hair.

I was forced to watch him choke the life out of my cat. Throwing his dead body into the front yard he looked down at me then spoke through clinched teeth,

"Are you happy now?"

Stepping back into the house he headed back towards their bedroom. I buried my head in my mom's side, my arms tight around her waist. My cat was just one of the many things Charles took from me.

My sister and I shared a room with two steel framed twin beds situated with one side pushed flush against the wall. This meant there was only one way of escape.

In the quiet darkness I heard him whisper my name. Dread prevented me from responding. Avoidance, the weapon I used to dodge his advances worked most of the time. But, his abuse even haunted my sleep.

Fifteen and angry about moving again, I started down a path that would bring unthinkable consequences.

Chapter 4

Eight wooden steps led to the door of our cramped two-bedroom trailer and to a life changing admission. Sunshine streamed pass the open kitchen curtains and cast a shadow of her coffee cup onto the darkly painted walls. Mom sat in one of the chairs around the dining table.

"Mom can I talk to you?"

"Sure, come sit down. How was school today?

"Ok"

"I know you don't like it here, but I need you to try."

"Alright mom"

Rapping my nails on the table, a habit triggered by anxiety and one my mother detested. She reached across the table and smashed my hand under her palm,

"STOP tapping your nails on the table. Is there something I can do for you Mary?"

"I missed my period"

"What?"

"I took a pregnancy test, it was positive."

I braced for impact. Nothing. She stared. I didn't dare turn my eyes away.

Two weeks later:

Sterile and cold, the Planned Parenthood clinic was the last place I wanted to be. My arm hurt from the grip she had on it. Mom made sure to hold tight to her prodigal child. The appointment had been made. I had no voice. My path had been chosen. The nurse called my name and my life would never be the same

Two years later, on their eighteenth wedding anniversary, Charles left.

Ruth struggled to provide for her four teenagers. The oldest, Mary, was on track to finish high school yet went missing for days at a time and had no time for her family. She was energetic, was lively, and had lots of friends, but she was more interested in playing than anything else. Mary would not take the word of anyone who pointed out possible consequences of her actions. The need to experience the results of her actions firsthand was a character trait that would haunt both mother and child for years. Deep in her heart Ruth knew choices she had made were to blame.

Chapter 5

Shakily she put the phone down. Dismay and grief made it hard to move. Unwelcome news from her oldest forced Ruth to make another difficult decision.

Recently engaged to her high school sweetheart Chip, Ruth hoped he would stop by on his way home from work. She heard the car door slam shut and ran to the front door. Without a word she hugged him so tight he gasped to get a breath. His smile faded and concern took over. Loosening her grip, Chip was able to ask,

"What is it, are the kids okay?"

Ruth just shook her head.

"I just got off the phone with Mary. She asked to come home and I told her no."

"Honey, did I do the right thing? I know she needs me, but it is beyond my capacity to save her one more time."

Telling Mary, she was not welcome at home when she was most in need was difficult. One grandchild in the house was enough. Most days it was difficult to see or comprehend God's plan for her or her children, but she held fast to the knowledge of a love that was beyond her understanding: God's love. Mary would likely hate her for being rejected, but Ruth put her on that plane for a reason.

Chapter 6

Relieved to be back on the ground, my first experience flying was not unpleasant. Compared to the forced submission which characterized my first year at college the summer after graduation, it was a fabulous trip.

"Just take a seat anywhere" a voice instructed with the help of a microphone. It was the first day of freshman orientation. The year, 1981. Excited and more than a little nervous, I listened as the speaker gave an overview of the upcoming week's activities. Convinced this new adventure would be the catalyst for change, I would do my best to get back on the right track.

Most of what was said did not register, except the mention of a swimming and pizza party on Friday evening. Determined to start fresh, the party on Friday would be the first step.

Several students milled around the dining table waiting for the pizza. Retreating some ways from the table, I looked around at my fellow Bible College students and felt like an outsider. Just weeks earlier, I had been out drinking, running around and hooking up with guys. Who was I trying to fool?

Picking at my pizza, I suddenly felt nauseous. New people and new surroundings were most likely to blame. A bug, it would pass. Alone in the crowd, I was unable to engage in a conversation. Relief returned as I stepped onto the campus van.

Lunchtime the following day my roommate suggested we go eat together.

"I feel awful and have been throwing up. Do you know if the school has a nurse?"

"I don't think we have a nurse, but Mrs. "H" can probably help."

"Thanks. Let's have lunch another time."

The next day, as soon as classes ended, I walked to the administration building. Approaching the receptionist, I asked if I could see Mrs. Hanlon.

"Take a seat and she will be with you as soon as she can."

I first met Mrs. Ilene Hanlon at freshmen orientation. The dean of women told us her previous job had been dorm mother at a college in Indiana. She also told the crowd that most students called her Mrs. H and she was okay with that.

An older woman with an infectious smile and kind eyes, she was always well-dressed and carried herself with grace. Her genuine concern for the students as well as her faith, was obvious.

Stepping out of her office Mrs. Hanlon greeted me with a warm and genuine smile, extended her hand, and cupped mine with both of hers.

"Come on in, sit down, and tell me your name."

"My name is Mary Roberts."

"How can I help you?"

"I have been feeling bad and throwing up. Is there was a nurse or someone who might be able to help?"

"We don't have a nurse on campus, but I would be happy to make an appointment for you to see a local doctor if you like."

"I don't have any money to pay for a doctor visit."

Mrs. "H" explained that payment for routine medical issues was part of the tuition.

In the waiting room of the doctor's office I stared at the carpet. Brandon crossed my mind. The unprotected sex we had may be the reason I felt so bad. Pushing that thought aside I heard my name being called.

Following the exam, the doctor gave no explanation. Maybe I should have asked more questions.

Later that week, on my way from the library, Mrs. Hanlon was walking towards me.

"Hello Mary, are you feeling any better"

"Hello, yes ma'am I am. Feeling better I mean."

"Would you have time now to speak with me in my office?"

"Yes, of course."

The sun was high in the sky, there were no visible clouds and despite the humidity, the temperatures were mild. Other students and faculty were also enjoying the perfect afternoon weather. The second time this week I followed Mrs. "H" into her office. Nervous, I was unprepared for the news she would give me.

The office was orderly and clean yet warm and welcoming. A big overstuffed chair sat in the corner and behind the desk was a big picture window.

"Sit down dear" Mrs. "H" said as she motioned to a chair directly in front of her desk.

"That is such a pretty skirt you are wearing!"

"Thank-you, my mom made it for me."

"Can I get you something to drink dear?"

"No, thank you."

"What I need to talk to you about is difficult. I must ask you a personal question.

"What about?"

"Is there a chance that you may be pregnant?"

"Why?"

"One of your test results came back positive for pregnancy. Now, sometimes these tests can be wrong."

"No, the test is not wrong."

Staring past her to the scene outside the window, it felt like someone punched me in the gut. The news rang in my ears like the clanging of church bells. Was this a bad dream? What was I going to do? My fresh start would have to wait, the consequences of past actions cannot be erased.

The tears that welled up in my eyes streamed down my cheeks. Reaching for a tissue from the box Mrs. "H" pushed towards me, I did my best not to make eye contact.

"I can't imagine what you must be going through right now.

"Try not to worry. The doctor calculates you are about 6 weeks along. Speak with your parents then let me know what they say so we can proceed. Be sure they understand that arrangements must be made for you to leave school."

Try not to worry, God has a way of working things out. I understand her intentions were to encourage. This was not the first time I had faced an unwanted pregnancy and nothing good had come out of either of those situations. I wanted to believe God could help but was unsure why he would.

Unable to speak through sobs, she waited for me to gain my composure. Oddly, there was never a feeling of judgement, only concern. Once I was able to speak more coherently, I thanked Mrs. "H" and apologized to her.

Through tears I cursed the sunshine and the warm air on the walk back to my room. Pregnant. Part of me wondered why it was such a shock. The same news had been delivered before.

Chapter 7

Ilene was not immune to the emotions that plague us all. Many nights, she dreaded going home to an empty house. The knowledge that God was her constant companion helped lessen the loneliness she lived with since her husband's death eight years earlier.

The key turned in the lock and Ilene hung her purse and sweater on the hook just inside the front door. Christmas break. A chance to rest and catch up on some reading.

An early dinner then to bed. Ilene planned to wake up and run errands early. The phone interrupted the silence. It was Hannah. Every year, together with family they attended Christmas Eve services. In recent years it was just the two of them. A friendship that had endured for more than thirty-five years of marriages, children, grandchildren, and the loss of their husbands.

Remembering how they met and how her life had been changed because of their friendship always brought a smile to Ilene's face. Hannah's husband had been the catalyst that helped her come to understand what true faith in Jesus meant.

Born on a farm in upstate New York, Ilene and her older brother lived there with their parents until Ilene married. After relocating to Ohio in 1945, Ilene and her husband of five years began attending a small country church outside Columbus. Teaching at a country school was a job she studied for. She had always wanted to work with students.

Hired in 1940 to pastor the church, he and his wife Hannah relocated from farmland in Pennsylvania. Close in age, Hannah and Ilene became friends and looked forward to seeing each other at church on Sundays

Church members visited in the foyer before the Sunday service. Making her way through the crowd to where she noticed Ilene. Once close enough, she gave her a hug.

"Are you coming to the meetings this week?"

"I want to, but I won't be able to make it until Friday night. I can't stay out late on a school night!"

The evening meeting was about to start. Together, Hannah and Ilene made their way to the front of the sanctuary and found seats in the third row. New faces were among those attending that Friday night.

Faithful to attend church Ilene thought of herself as a "good" person. A heartfelt belief in Jesus Christ is the only way to be truly saved. These verses were familiar, but she understood them for the first time. Knowing about Jesus is not the same and knowing who he is, and Ilene wanted to know Him in a personal way.

One of the first ones to make her way down the aisle, Ilene was not worried what others thought. Believing she would never be good enough to earn God's favor, she needed a savior. As she knelt on the steps of the stage pastor asked her why she had come forward. She wanted to know Jesus as her savior. She believed he was the son of God and the only way to God. In the spring of 1945, Ilene came to know Jesus in a personal way.

The friendship between Ilene and Hannah continued to grow. Friends through pregnancies, trials and loss. Hannah's last child Evelyn was born in 1953. A life-long friendship would soon be the key to rescue an unborn child.

Chapter 8

The church located near the College provided the spiritual food Edward and his growing family needed. More than excellent Bible teaching, the members went out of their way to welcome them as part of their family of believers. Not long after Ed and his family became members the church family prayed asking the Lord to send a youth pastor to be on staff full-time. Ed wondered if Will might consider a move.

Will, the pastor of a small church in Montana. His first job after finishing his Master of Divinity at the college where Ed currently worked.

Ed was fifteen when William was born. Will, outspoken and rebellious, concealed a wild side. Ed, older and less impulsive had been a positive influence to help keep his friend Will headed in the right direction. Like Ed's mentor, Pastor Howard Sr., had done for him.

As Will put on his coat the phone rang.

"Hello, this is Pastor Howard."

"Hey there, how are things in Montana?"

"Ed, it's good to hear from you. I am on my way out how can I help you?"

"I will be quick. Our church here in Atlanta has been praying to ask the Lord for a new youth pastor. The school year will start soon, and I hoped you might consider the opportunity. The most anxious for a new youth leader are my own kids. I have been filling in."

Will enjoyed living close to Ed and his family in Atlanta and leading the youth. The opportunity had been something he would cherish, but he missed pastoring a church. A position for a senior pastor was available. The small town in rural Georgia, would be the next step for Will. Shepherding the flock in that small church would prove to be the most rewarding and the most challenging job he would face as a pastor.

The small mining community was home. Shade trees and open spaces made his daily walks comfortable. A closeness to God had developed as Will spent time in the splendor of creation. The crisp fall day beckoned to him from his office in the church.

Coming in from a longer than usual walk he tried to shake off the cold. The cooler weather hinted of changing seasons. Will immediately noticed the message light blinking on the phone and wondered who might have called him. Listening to the message he realized it was from one of his good friends.

"Hey Willie! Ed Thomas here, I need to talk to you about something. Please give me a call as soon as you can. God Bless."

'Willie' the word brought a smile to his face. The only person who ever called him that was Ed. The vagueness of the message piqued his interest.

That week, at Sunday morning service, Pastor Howard announced there would be a special meeting of the membership Tuesday evening. He asked them to pray for the Lord's guidance and leading. There was speculation as to the urgency for an unscheduled meeting.

Most of the members sat near the front of the sanctuary quietly pondering the news.

"Thank-you all for being here this evening, I need to share a situation with you. As a Christian congregation who desire to follow Christ, I ask you to carefully consider what, if anything, we can do to help.

A longtime friend of mine, Edward Thomas, dean of students at an Atlanta Bible College called me this past week and asked for prayer for a student who has just found out she is pregnant. Whatever the reasons, her parents are unable or unwilling to take her in. Let's prayerfully consider how our church family might help this student. With no financial support this young lady has no place to go."

Chapter 9

Pregnant again. Self-hate and dread made hard work of the walk to my dorm room. The key turned in the lock. Grateful my roommate wasn't there. Once in my room, the tears flowed like a swift moving river. I lie down on my bed and fell asleep.

"Collect call from Mary, will you accept?"

"Yes!"

"Hi sweetheart, how are you doing? It is so good to hear from you."

"I wanted to let you know I was chosen to sing with the ladies' choir, and I have made lots of friends. I am so glad to be here!"

"That is so great!" We need to discuss you coming home for Thanksgiving. It will be so good to hear about all you are learning and about all of your friends."

"Got to run, someone is knocking on my door."

"Bye-bye honey. Talk to you later, love you!"

"Love you too mom!"

A knock on the door of my room woke me. Amanda, my new friend, stopped by to see if I was ready for dinner.

"It's taco Tuesday tonight. Let's go before they run out."

"I'm not hungry and I just woke up. You go ahead without me."

"You want me to bring you something?"

"No, thank-you though, I can last till breakfast. See you then?"

Locking the door behind her, I sat on the edge of the bed and remembered my dream. If only dreams could come true. The last thing I wanted to do was call home. Putting it off would not make it easier.

"Operator I have a collect call from Mary will you accept the charges?"

18

Unsure what to say or how to say it, a piercing chill came over me when I heard mom's voice.

"Yes. Yes, I will"

"Hi honey. How are you?

"Hi Mom, I'm fine."

"How's everyone there?"

"Good, the baby is walking, and your sister is a great mom even though she is young. Having a baby around is hard, but we are making it."

"That's great."

Mom rattled on about something and interrupting would add to her disappointment. The possibility she might leave me hanging was real. Mom stopped chattering; knowing I was too quiet,

"Are you alright Mary?

"I need to come home."

"Why? Don't you like it there?"

"Yes! I do. That's not it."

"Then why would you want to leave?"

"The week after I arrived, I started throwing up. The college paid for me to go see a doctor and…

I'm pregnant and need to come home"

Silence as heavy and dark as the night sky. Had she hung up on me?

"Are you still there?"

"Yes, I'm here"

"Please mom, I need your help."

The words rang in her mind over and over, "I'm pregnant and need to come home"

"Honey, I am sorry, what do you want me to say?"

"Tell me you will buy me a plane ticket home."

"Mary, I just can't have you at home if you are pregnant. It is something I can't handle right now. You will have to make other arrangements."

"But mom, what am I supposed to do?"

"I don't know, just try to understand my position."

"What about my position?"

Chapter 10

A picture window let ample light into the reception area just outside her office. I waited. Mrs. "H" called my name from the doorway. "Hello dear, come in and sit down."

Mrs. Hanlon, Ilene, motioned for me to sit in the comfy overstuffed chair in the corner of her office. Once we were both seated, she smiled and asked;

"Were you able to speak with your mother?"

"Yes, she told me I can't come home because she couldn't deal with it right now. I know I can't stay here."

"Things look bleak now, but Dean Thomas and I will do everything we can to help you. In the meantime, you will still attend classes. It would be best if you did not say anything to the other students."

Continue to attend classes and pretend nothing was wrong. A skill I learned at an early age. However, there was no plan when I considered my uncertain future. God was not done with me and gave me a glimpse of how he loves through his people in that meeting with the Dean of students.

Humble, approachable, and soft spoken, Edward Thomas was respected by both students and faculty. A brilliant man, he often spoke in chapel services. The placard on the door read Dean of Students. Floor to ceiling bookcases lined two walls of the modestly furnished office. Seated on a leather couch, myself and Mrs. "H" listened as he explained about a Christian family who had offered me a place to live while I waited for the baby to be born.

"These people don't know me, why would they want to help?"

"Mrs. Hanlon shared your situation. Prayerfully, we considered ways to help. I called a pastor friend. His congregation decided they want to help you. One, an Obstetrician, will monitor the pregnancy; another, a Christian counselor, has offered to see you on a weekly basis, free of charge; and yet another member of the church, a young mom and midwife is looking forward to meeting you and helping prepare you for birth. These Saints recognize we all make mistakes. Sin and its consequences plague us all. Concern for you and the baby is why they want to help you."

Eight weeks pregnant, grateful for a place to live and for my friend Amanda. Red hair and blue eyes she walked alongside me, made me laugh and helped me feel a sense of joy. The reality of my condition was momentarily forgotten. Thanksgiving with Amanda's family was a bright spot in a bleak season. Chocolate covered pretzels were the star of the week.

God shows us love in so many ways. A sunset, a smile, a friend to walk beside you; a family who gives up space, time and comfort to help a young girl they don't know.

Chapter 11

Miles of cotton fields and small farms dotted the landscape on the drive to our new home. The mid-afternoon sun peaked out from behind a cloud as we parked in the drive. A pungent odor greeted us when we stepped from the car. Introductions were made. Mr. and Mrs. Patterson owned several acres and ran a pig farm. The reason for the smell.

He wore a ball cap. A toothpick hung halfway out of his mouth.

"You'll eventually get used to the smell."

Honest concern and kindness were all I ever received from this man. She wore an apron.

The staircase to the newly remodeled loft was narrow, but the bedroom spacious. Gratitude washed over me. A pile of clothes was laid on the freshly made bed.

"We gathered maternity clothes for you to use for the next few months. We figured you would need some."

Weeks earlier I was facing homelessness. Is this what real love looks like? Discouragement left me feeling empty. My faith was weak. The realization that someone could love me began to break down the wall of distrust and doubt that encompassed my heart. Members of a small church in rural Georgia had given us a second chance.

Chapter 12

The first of several pre-arranged appointments with the counselor felt like a waste of time.

"Mr. Griffin is ready to see you now. Right this way please."

"Come in and sit down. I am Miles Griffin, the counselor Pastor Howard told you about and we will be meeting together once a week for the next few months."

"Hi. I have never talked to a "*shrink*" before, how does this work?

He just smiled at me and said nothing. Uncomfortable with the silence,

"Why do I have to come see you anyway? No offense, but how is talking to you supposed to help me?"

"Good question. Do you think you need help?"

His comment lined up with stereotypical jabs about therapists. He was content to sit in silence and wait. The hour crawled by. A name with initials behind it did not ease my discomfort to share personal stuff.

Gazing out of the waiting room window, I noticed a butterfly flitting about. Odd, it's January. It rested on a tree branch between flights. I flashed back to that evening and the overwhelming desperation and anger after the phone call with my mother.

The smell of newly laid turf accosted my senses. I hugged my knees to my chest. Tears would not stop. Disbelief and self-loathing clung to me like moss to a rock. I wanted everything to go back to the way it was two days earlier. Standing up I ran as fast as I could around the track until I collapsed. Exhaustion did not create rest. Loud thoughts mocked me, 'How are you going to have a baby? Where will you live? You have no money, no job and the people you know here will not help you if they found out your secret. After all you are supposed to be a Christian.' Jab after jab, my thoughts beat me up. The mad voice in my head was right. Suicide was an option. I would not fail a second time.

A quiet yet distinct voice told me to hold on. Be still, somehow, someway things would be handled. Listening to the voice I clung to a weak thread of faith.

The door to the office closed shut. Mrs. Patterson stood there then I heard her sweet voice, "Mary, are you ready to go?"

Chapter 13

Private adoption, an option the couple never considered. A college student willing to give up her baby and it would be handled privately.

"Don't let the stack of paperwork scare you, most of it is easily explained. This is the first time you have pursued a private adoption, correct?

"Yes, that is correct. Applying through state agencies we were unaware it was an option for us."

"This first meeting is preliminary. At our next meeting, I need you to bring two things. Firstly, you need to provide me with some character references. Secondly, a letter explaining why you feel you will be good parents. References and the letter will be given to the birth mother. However, since this is a closed adoption all names and dates will be blacked out.

The due date is not for three months but, legally the birth mother has five days after giving birth to change her mind. A remote possibility, but still a possibility."

First time moms rarely deliver on the due date. That date had come and gone yet still no word. Anxious for a call with any news about the baby, the ringing was a welcome sound.

Evelyn answered the phone,

"Hello?"

"Hello, this is the lawyer, Miles Clark"

"Hi, Mr. Clark do you have news for us?'

"Yes, but probably not the news you were hoping for. The baby has not been born yet. Just wanted to let you know the birth mother will have her labor induced next week. It can sometimes take many hours for the baby to be born when this type of procedure is done. There is no need to worry. Someone will call you as soon as we get word of the delivery."

Chapter 14

Groggy and unable to feel anything from the waist down due to an epidural, I heard a voice say, "It's a girl."

Noticeable annoyed, the nurse stopped mid stride when I asked to see my baby. The newborn turned her head toward my voice and her beautiful blue eyes looked right at me. Many decisions and events of the last few years flashed through my mind like the reel of a silent movie.

It was mid-April 1982.

Tears slid down my face as I watched the door close behind the nurse. The pain of loss was intense. Sarah came around the table and put a reassuring hand on my shoulder. Had it not been for her, I would have been alone.

Word of the delivery came early the next morning, just hours after the birth. A smile brightened her face. She pinched herself then shouted at the top of her lungs.

A knock at the door interrupted the joyous moment.

"Hello George, is everything ok?"

"I'm here to ask you the same thing. I heard a loud shout and came to check that you are ok"

"I am so happy, we have a baby girl, Grace"

Hours after giving birth, regret set in. My decision not to hold the child is one I still regret. If do-overs were possible, I would have held her every minute possible for those first five days regardless of the pain of letting go.

Forty-eight hours later I was back at the home where I lived for the past five months. This home was not tucked away under some inauspicious name, it belonged to the most selfless and hardworking people. This farm family had lovingly, with no expectation of reciprocation, provided me with food, clothing and a warm place to live during my pregnancy despite the reason that brought me there. The only one who ever passed judgment on me was-myself.

Chapter 15

The Patterson's took their usual seats near the front of the sanctuary; I sat down in the back. The last Sunday attending a church where the godliest and faithful believers worshipped. Two rows behind the Patterson's sat one woman who most impacted my life during the past five months. Sarah, an amazing woman and midwife with an infectious smile; a wonderful wife and mother and someone who cared about me. Sarah helped me give birth and aided in my rebirth.

Dinner that afternoon included fried chicken and homemade apple pie. The food was always delicious and abundant. Once the dishes were cleared and washed, I took a walk. The time lived in the Georgia countryside had been some of the best and hardest of my life.

Later in the afternoon while reading on my bed, Mrs. Patterson knocked on the open door of my room.

"Come on in, I was just reading."

Caring, soft spoken, hardworking and loving. This woman had been like a mother. On my last day with them she was concerned for my well-being.

"Are you sure you are ready to go back to College?"

"Yes, why?"

"It has only been a few weeks since you had the baby. Maybe you should consider going home and work on reconciling things with your mom."

The way things were between my mother and I suited me. The heavy burden of the baby recently born and given away would not be lifted easily.

The small window in the attic room looked out on the manicured lawn. A smile broke through as I remembered Mrs. Patterson teaching me to bake cookies.

"How do you make your cookies so soft?"

"I will let you in on one of my secrets. You make the cookies 'sad'."

"Sad?"

"To make every batch soft and chewy drop the cookie sheet on the counter once you take it out of the oven. You see how the cookies become flat and 'sad' when I do this?"

"Yes but, I think I need to test one to be sure it worked."

Grateful seems too mild an accolade to this family who made room for me, allowed me to live in their house, fed me and drove me to work and church. They had rescued me and my unborn child. They saved our lives. All other gestures of kindness were like adding sprinkles to your frosted cupcake.

Patterson's gave me a ride back to school. The college approved my return, gave me a job and a room for the summer. I cleaned the women's bathrooms in the one dormitory in use for the summer. An offer to work graveyard at the switchboard was proposed. Mrs. "H" knew it was difficult for me financially.

Two part-time jobs and a full class load began to take its toll. Eight weeks into the semester the switchboard job ended. Barely scraping by with one job and exhausted, change was inevitable.

The month-long Christmas break was approaching. Mom and I did not talk much. Would she understand that studying music was her dream and not the best plan for me? Desperate for redemption from past mistakes and the weight of the previous years' events; a new start may help.

"Of course, I will stay in touch. You have been a lifesaver. I can never repay all that you and the college have done for me."

Gospel music played on the radio and the traffic was light.

"May I ask you something?"

"Yes"

"Do you know the people who adopted my baby?"

"Yes"

"Will you stay in contact with them?"

"I plan to."

"Would it be okay, when I write, to ask about my little girl? Can you please let me know how she is doing as she grows up?"

"Of course, you can be sure that I will also keep your confidence. You are stronger than you believe, and the Lord will give you strength when you need it if you remember to ask Him."

"I feel so blessed to have met you. Thank-you again for everything."

Mrs. "H" watched the young lady leave her office and smiled to herself. Ilene would get to watch the little girl grow and be a part of her life, since her best friend was the child's grandmother.

Chapter 16

The night was cold, the darkness heavy. Slowly fastening my seatbelt, we drove toward our destination. A familiar uneasiness settled in my stomach and jumbled thoughts made me hesitate to say anything but, I knew that Kyle had to be told.

Four months earlier Kyle and I started dating. Most of the time we had fun together but there were fights; lots of fights. Secretly, I hoped he would walk away and leave me to care for my child on my own. However, God showed himself faithful once again.

Our first Christmas as a married couple and parents of a three-month-old was exhausting. The New Year was underway, and we looked forward to a few days of rest and quiet. The ringing phone woke us. It was nearly midnight.

Mom rarely called and never so late. My immediate thought was someone in the family was hurt or worse.

"Mom? Are you alright?"

"Yes, I am fine and so is Papa."

Relieved, I was able to breathe easier.

She continued,

"I need to let you know Charles is dead. He committed suicide."

I stared at the wall ahead of me for several seconds, then acknowledged what she told me. A domestic dispute between he and his fiancé escalated and he threatened to kill himself. With gun in hand and police officers at the ready, he turned the gun on himself. He died December 28, 1984.

The tangle of emotions included, of all things, sadness. The man, who belittled, abused and never said a kind or uplifting word to me, was dead. Why should I care? The truth is I loved him. He was never the dad I wanted or needed but he was still my dad. My tears were for innocence lost as well as the loss of a life.

Born September of 1984 six months after we were married, our daughter Deborah was beautiful. The love we had for our little girl made life seem less crazy. The simple life and plans we had made ended when Kyle joined the military.

Pregnant with baby number two, the military paid health care for active duty service members and their families.

December 1986, we welcomed our son Matthew to the world. He arrived early morning on the 28th.

Chapter 17

Drinking and nightly doses of sleeping pills led to an incident that would shatter my marriage and alter life forever. Our relationship was always unstable. Marriage was proposed out of responsibility and "*doing the right thing.*" Mutual love and respect were not reflected in our life together. Stationed where the climate is mild year-round and near several beaches, our circle of friends loved to party. Once the uniform came off, out came the booze. Drinking had again become a daily ritual. Truth lurked in drunken inhibitions.

Alcohol inhibited my weak and wavering faith. Plagued by the need for love and attention, flirtatious described my actions when drinking. The strain on my marriage continued. The more I drank the worse tensions between Kyle and me.

One summer evening while drinking with friends I tried to kiss another man in sight of my husband. The door slammed, Kyle lapped the parking lot honking the horn and cursing. The reflection in the mirror was one I recognized but chose to ignore. I stepped out of the bathroom; I did not care what these people thought of me.

The beach supported the heavy weight I carried. Instantly the father of my children and husband was changed by my uninhibited confession of other encounters. The silence between us was deafening.

Pounding his fist on the sand,

"Why? Why would you do that to me?"

Once sober, I would try to answer his question. Hearing my voice was not what he needed.

Threats to take the children, although harsh, was the catalyst for me to enroll in an outpatient treatment program where I began learning how to live without alcohol. The marriage survived and the next summer we had orders to another duty station.

Chapter 18

Sobriety is difficult when dealing with past mistakes. One of the ways to stay on the right path is attending Alcoholics Anonymous (AA) and church regularly. One year sober when we arrived in Arizona, the AA group was my lifeline.

The Women's ministry at our church also proved vital to my sobriety. The guilt of two abortions five years apart seemed unforgivable. The truth discovered in a Bible study titled *Post Abortion Counseling Education PACE* - would help me begin to heal.

The first night of the study the leader asked those of us who would like to, to share how we came to know Jesus. Sharing my story was crucial for me. Raising my hand, I started;

"My name is Mary. I used to think I was saved because I recited a prayer when I was young, but I found out years later that was not the case.

Two months after a failed suicide attempt, I sat in class at Bible College. The answer to the question I struggled with for years would be answered by the professor.

'I am sure some of you in here believe you are a Christian because some time in your life you said a prayer. Although it was prayed in all sincerity, the act of saying a prayer is not what saves you. It is believing that Jesus died on the cross for your sins and that he is alive and can live in you. The words of your prayer are telling God you believe who he is and that he has the power to change you.'

I bowed my head right then and told God I believed, then asked him to live in me and change me. That was how I came to know who Jesus is."

Holding onto the guilt of my actions pushed me into behaviors which temporarily numbed the pain yet placed me farther from the redemption God provides through Jesus.

Finding freedom from self-hatred and forgiveness through the PACE Bible Study would allow me to help other girls and women suffering the pain and loss due to abortion.

Chapter 19

April each year my spirits would fall. The pain from losing my first born became fresh again. 1996, mid-April, somewhere a young lady, who shared my DNA was turning sixteen. How would she celebrate her birthday?

In previous years, to lessen the pain I would pour myself a stiff drink. Sober five years, that was not an option, so I wrote her a letter.

'To my daughter,

I remember the day you were born and there are so many things I wish I could tell you. I love you although I am sure you wonder how that could be true. I know you are a beautiful girl and I trust you are doing well in school.'

Our living apart has provided a fuller life for you and given you things I would not have been able to give. I am married now; we have two kids.

My favorite color is purple what is yours? Do you love chocolate as much as I do?'

Carefully, I placed the notebook in the drawer, the door closed behind him; Kyle was home early.

"I got orders today."

"Where are we headed next?"

"Europe."

The journey was not over. Another adventure was on the horizon. New experiences, new friendships and new insights.

Chapter 20

The kids' father met us at the airport. The dog was ecstatic to see her "man." Lying down and napping for one or two days, was forefront in my mind. Readjusting to the many hours' time difference would happen sooner if we waited to sleep until later in the day. The flight was over, and we were home.

Blossoms dotted the countryside. Knee high grasses breathed in the sunshine. Kyle had found a house outside the military base. The rental was owned by a wonderful couple. The most beautiful wood cabinets hung in the kitchen, even the door of the refrigerator wood. The polished wood floors were so shiny one could see their reflection. Our landlord was gracious and meek, yet a physically strong man. He was a master gardener and always shared the fruits of his labor with us. There is nothing like fresh zucchini on the grill.

June was hot. The cost of electricity was prohibitive. No air conditioning meant a different way of cooling our home. Our landlord explained how to keep the house cool.

"Rise early in the morning, open the wooden shutters on the screenless windows to let in the cool morning air. When the temperatures start heating up, close the shutters and use as little light as possible."

This worked well until about noon, when the 90-degree heat and humidity made it unbearable to be inside.

One of our first purchases, four inexpensive bicycles. School was out for summer and the heat had us riding to the pool three or four days a week.

Her thick, curly black hair was unmanageable in the heat and humidity. Drawn to her smile I introduced myself.

"Hello, my name is Mary; it seems our kids have hit it off."

"Military kids are good at making new friends quickly."

Sitting at the small round plastic table shaded by a too small of an umbrella, within earshot of our kids, Christine asked,

"How long have you been here?

"We just arrived the first of June and live off post."

She and her husband of fifteen years had three kids. Twins, a boy and a girl. The oldest, a girl, was the same age as Deborah. Her husband planned to retire as did mine. Her husband worked on military vehicles, mine worked as a medic.

Chapter 21

Arriving on time, I made my way to an open door which faced the parking lot. Surprised at the number of ladies in the room, I noticed the coffee and pastries. A cup of coffee in hand, I found a seat near the front. Several women introduced themselves and welcomed me.

"We are waiting for our 'fearless leader' to arrive," one of the ladies explained after introducing herself. There was a *ruckus* in the back of the room I turned to see her carrying several bags and a poster. She nearly stumbled as she made her way to the front of the room. Smiling like she meant it, Christine was their "fearless leader." Quirky and fun loving, Christine came into my life. With no expectation for the friendship, something wonderful happened.

Christine led the local Protestant Women of the Chapel (PWOC) group with grace, love, and laughter. In the span of eighteen months, Christine and I forged a lifetime bond. We shared similar struggles physically and emotionally. Victory was found in our relationship with Jesus.

Preparations for Chapel sponsored trips fell to the active duty chaplain on staff. Annual PWOC conferences were held in Germany. A two-day trip in a sixteen-passenger van.

"Ladies, can I have your attention please? The conference is two weeks out. The van has been rented, arrangements for your lodging has been finalized. Please note you must provide your own food for the trip until you reach the conference center. Show of hands if you can drive a vehicle with a standard transmission. Christine was the only driver last year; it would be good to have others to help."

Out of fifteen women one hand went up. Mine.

The drive across Germany was picturesque. Houses with the same color roof tiles. Orderly, and clean. Quaint towns with amazing architecture. Excitement overrode the tiredness. When we arrived, check-in was as neat and orderly as the country.

"I can't believe tomorrow is our last day. What a great week it's been."

"Mary, there is one more person we still need to prank. I need your help."

"Who's there?"

"It's Mary."

"Door is open come on in."

I hoped she didn't notice the mischievous look in my eye.

You still want to go to the pool?"

"Yes, I do"

"Ok, Christine will meet us there."

The last one to arrive at breakfast the next morning was our Area President.

Calmly, Sherry hung her bag on the back of the chair.

"Good morning girls.

There was no way she could have missed the door decoration. The suspense was killing me.

"Anything new to report?"

"Besides the cow suit Christine is wearing, I found a lovely maxi pad wreath on my door."

We laughed until our sides hurt.

It had been a wonderful week of classes, pranks, great food and laughter.

Later in the day we would venture back home.

Chapter 22

O ur journeys were similar. One of a few people who knew the truth about my past. God used Christine to show me others too, make poor choices, but those choices do not have to define you. Memories of the dysfunction that characterized my upbringing would rush back with a song or a scent. The radio was my companion each afternoon when I picked the kids up from afterschool ball practice.

"This next song is brought to you by Armed Forces Europe Radio. The classic hit, 'Stairway to Heaven.'"

June 1979. The scholarship arrived in the mail two days earlier.

"It's a full ride to a college nearby. Isn't that great?"

"Mary, forget the scholarship, you are going to a Bible College in Illinois."

"Illinois, why?"

Short on answers it was decided. The trip was a long and silent one. Mom and her boyfriend took turns driving.

Luggage dotted the sidewalk outside the entrance to the administration building. One car after another, students waved as their parents drove away. The car pulled away from the curb. I turned my back as she drove away.

Startled back to the present with a knock on the window.

"Mom, open the door. Practice is over."

"Seatbelt"

"Can you drop me by Zoey's she wants me to spend the night?"

"Ok."

Music and the sound of kids laughing could be heard through the open door.

"Knock, knock, Christine?"

Chapter 23

One year later, we left Europe. Our new place in Arizona was nice, but I missed Christine. I picked up the phone and dialed her number.

"How are you doing my friend?"

"Hey there, we are doing well"

"How are your kids?"

"Good, we really like it here in Arizona, but we miss you guys terribly."

"We miss you guys too."

"So, anything new to report?"

"We found a good church and Zoey graduates next year."

"Deborah is graduating also. One down, one to go!"

"And, the twins, how are they doing?"

"They are great. Still getting good grades and making lots of friends."

Phone calls, e-mails and text messages kept the friendship strong. However, over time, communication became less frequent. I was overjoyed to hear her voice on the phone one evening in 2006.

"Hello?"

"Hi this is Christine!"

"What a great surprise. How are you guys?"

"Doing well, I have some news to tell you."

"My husband has decided to retire."

"Awesome! Will you stay there or move?"

"We love it here and are considering staying. We own our home and have our pets. Our church is the biggest reason we don't want to leave. The cost of college tuition is another. Zoey is attending classes at the University of Atlanta and the twins are planning to go there as well. We can save money if they live at home while they take classes. Also, a dear friend of mine lives here. We met when she spoke at a Women's retreat at church two years ago. I think I told you about her."

"I remember you telling me about that weekend."

"I hope to introduce you to her one day."

"I would love to meet her."

In less than five years our lives would become entwined in ways we could never have imagined.

Chapter 24

The end of another week-long work conference in San Diego, California. A two-hour drive north my sister owned a home and planned to drive down for the weekend.

Moments before a message came through on the company issued iPhone my sister stepped out to get some ice. Crumpled on the floor next to the bed, crying uncontrollably, she helped me onto the bed.

"What's wrong, what happened?"

Nothing coherent came out of my mouth. I handed her the phone. Tears fell as she read.

The room seemed eerily bright, yet objects were hazy. Pacing back and forth in the hotel room with a smile on my face and a knot in my stomach, I tried to wrap my head around the content of the e-mail message from Christine.

> 'What I have to share with you is pretty far out. I have had a week to process this and yet my feet have not touched the ground. You see what I am going to share has God's ordaining ALL over it. I could not fathom a more spectacular story. What God creates in the stories of human life supersedes our limited ability to be truly amazing. Here goes the amazing- please sit down:
>
> On a Saturday afternoon 1/22 I got a text from a young lady named Grace. She is the daughter of a friend of mine, Evelyn, who I have known for about 7 years. Grace is also a friend

of Zoey's. Grace's husband Peter was in a band with Zoey's husband years ago.

Grace asked me in the text if I knew you and Matthew and how. I was stunned at the randomness of such a question. I shared by text how I knew you and I asked her why she was asking. She then called me and asked if she could come see me.

Two hours later Grace arrived with her husband Peter. She sat down and began to explain that she found your son Matthew on Facebook and noticed you on his page. She handed me a small stack of letters and a couple photos. Mary, Grace told me that she has been searching for you as long as she can remember. The letters I was looking at were in your handwriting. The two photos were of you with Mrs. "H" at the Patterson's' home. Grace believes you are her biological mother.

Grace had been searching Facebook for a while. She had your last name spelled wrong. When she discovered her error and corrected the misspelling that is when she pulled up Matthew's page. This all happened on the Saturday she called me.

Are you ok? Grace was shocked to see Zoey's and my photo on Matthew's Facebook page as mutual friends. None of us had ANY idea about any of this. I can tell you that my family, along with Grace and hers, are in shock. And now, I assume you are too.

(I return to Psalm 139 over and over this past week. God HAS ordained ALL your days. He saw the day you gave birth to a baby you never knew. ALL the days leading up to these days. This day, this moment.)

Mary, are you ok? I will tell you that it has been the utmost concern for Grace that this news not hurt you. Grace's parents, Larry and Evelyn Davidson also want this to be redemptive news for you. You have been prayed for and you are deemed with great respect and gratitude from this family. They have loved you from afar. Grace asked me to contact you not wanting to corner you. She spent all week long, since finding you on Facebook, praying and discerning how best to make contact with you. Again, her concern is for you.

I want to share something important; Grace wants you to understand that the woman who supported you during your pregnancy and organized the adoption, Mrs. "H" has never shared any information regarding your identity. She has honored your wishes to remain anonymous and guarded your information well.

Mary, I can only imagine the shock you must be experiencing. Like I said earlier I have had a week to process this. No other way to put this other than "mind blowing". For His purposes. He has invited my family to be part of this story. I did not see this coming. I am still awestruck. So, do you want to call me? You can. What can I do for you? Please let me know. I am praying, praying, praying for your dear heart. Mary, you are loved, loved, loved.

I will close with this. It is Grace's desire to meet you, but only if that is also your desire. She wants the very best for you Mary. She is a lovely woman, just like you, just like Deborah. She loves Jesus! God has done a good work in this girl who wants so much for your peace and well-being. Her parents too desire blessing for you. All these years, love, prayer and blessing have been sent your way by this family.'

Caught up in a miracle-

Back home daily conversations with my husband Antonio would focus on how unreal and "random" the situation seemed and my decision to meet her.

"Do you want to meet Grace?"

"I am still not sure. Maybe once I talk with Christine, I can make a decision."

Two weeks passed before I mustered the courage to dial her number.

"How are you?" I asked my friend.

"I am fine, but the real question is how YOU are doing?"

"I must have read your e-mail a hundred times. Very graciously written, thank-you for that."

"Your welcome. I can only imagine what you must be feeling. She has been looking for her birth mom for a long time and really believes you are her. The evidence is overwhelming!"

That was for sure.

"Christine, do you believe she would understand if I decide not to speak with her? How do her parents feel about this? Have you talked with her since you sent the e-mail?"

My words ran together like the juice from a medium rare burger running into the fries on your plate.

"I am so sorry for rambling and all the questions. I am still in shock. Many times, I picked up the phone but was unsure I was ready for what might follow when I finally dialed."

Christine assured me Grace's concern was genuine, and she would understand whatever I decided.

"I told Grace I would call her as soon as I heard anything from you. She has been so anxious she has called me every day for the past two weeks. She will be so happy that you did. If she calls me again, is it okay to give her your phone number?"

I hesitated; if I told her no it would be over, and life could go on as it had before. Should I agree and she contacted me what would that look like?

"Yes, that would be fine. I am still amazed that she tried so hard to find her "bio" mom. What are the chances that you and her mom would become friends, and that she and Zoey would meet on the campus at Georgia State? How in the world did all this happen?

"There is only one way all the pieces came together the way they have. God designed it to happen decades ago."

Chapter 25

Caller ID showed a call from Atlanta. On the fourth ring I snatched up the receiver

"Hello?"

"Hello, could I speak to Mary please?"

"This is she."

"Hi Mary, this is Grace!"

Speechless is not a word used to describe me. However, for several seconds no words came.

Finally, my voice squeaked out a weak "Hi, I don't really know what to say to you."

"I understand, but I want you to know I have looked for my birth mom most of my life. Talking to her, connecting with her, is something I have dreamed of.

"I imagined you would be angry with the woman who gave you up."

"Not at all, my parents made sure my birth mom was part of every birthday celebration."

"It is unexpected that your parents are accepting of you finding your birth mom."

"My mom encouraged me to contact you."

"Oh."

"I was wondering if you have any information on my "bio" dad?"

"No, I remember is his first name and some physical characteristics. He was tall, maybe 6 ft. 4 inches and we worked together at an arcade in Tampa the summer before I went back to College."

"Did his family live in Florida?"

"I don't know that either, I hardly knew him. We only went out once and I never saw him again."

"I have so many questions but would rather ask you face-to-face. We lived in Colorado for a while and I graduated from high school there. My husband, Peter and I have been talking about taking time off and visiting the Rockies. If we did that, what would you think about meeting in person?"

"How long have you been married?"

"A year in July. We met in college. That's where I met Zoey. Christine, her mom, is friends with my mom. So, what do you think about meeting in person?! Do you feel comfortable with that? I am guessing you may need to think about it, right?"

"Let me talk with my husband and I'll let you know the next time we talk."

"One more thing, mom would like to write to you."

"I would like that."

Taken back by the seemingly random connections of people and places and how truly amazing a story this was. Grace was likely a part of me, and the opportunity to get to know her was real.

Chapter 26

The anticipation of meeting Grace for the first time and a strong tug at my heart fueled research into the local Crisis Pregnancy center and the possibility of volunteering.

A three-ring binder under my arm I waited for the elevator after day one of volunteer orientation. Ground level of our apartment building housed 60 mailboxes that covered more than half a wall. The handwritten return address on the only piece of mail made my stomach flip. It was from Grace! I suppressed the urge to rip the letter open. Something inside the note card fell onto the rug underneath the kitchen table. Return address labels.

Her note contained questions and facts from her childhood. She also wrote 'I want you to know, I understand you gave me up out of love, not shelfishness.'

She expressed excitement about our meeting.

The newlyweds checked into a hotel near the Denver Airport only ten-minutes by car to our downtown Condo. Concerned there may be hard feelings, family members offered advice on the best course of action for this type of reunion.

"It is recommended you have a third-party present when meeting for the first time."

"Dad, I know you mean well, but I'm not sure that will be necessary."

My father-in-law, a Psychologist, knew from experience these meetings can be less than amiable.

Prayer and re-reading Grace's letter along with a letter from her mom calmed my fears. Unaccompanied, we would meet face-to-face."

The card made of white handmade paper decorated with dried leaves and a bunch of tiny rose buds tied with string, contained a handwritten note. The words on the linen paper were words of true love for Grace and gratefulness to God. Evelyn wrote that she was glad Grace and I would meet soon.

'Not just for Grace but, for "all of us. I have prayed for your meeting and that aching questions be met and answered.'

Chapter 27

I circled the parking lot and found an empty parking space. The crisp spring air grazed my face as I locked my car. The restaurant, located near the Cherry Creek, was one of my favorites. Several ducks floated on the water that day, their white tail feathers contrasted beautifully against the blue sky. A serene scene, unlike the flutter of emotions I was experiencing. On the slow walk toward the entrance my mind replayed the one question I hoped she would not ask.

The hostess greeted me; "welcome, would you like a table or a booth?"

"A booth please"

Located near the back of the restaurant, the booth was not visible from the front entrance. The roomy, padded leather bench held my sweater and purse. I laid my phone on the table and placed my folded hands on top of the unopened menu.

When the waitress approached the table, I told her I was waiting for someone. However, to give my shaky hands something besides each other to hold, I ordered a diet soda and water with lemon.

"I will be right back with that."

The knot in my stomach grew larger and more uncomfortable with each sip of my drink. The imminent meeting had life changing potential.

"Can I get you another diet rite?" the waitress interrupted my thoughts.

"Yes, thank-you, it should only be a few more minutes before she gets here."

A phone conversation two hours earlier confirmed she was excited to meet. The alarm on my phone signaled it was time. A vehicle pulled into a parking spot as I stood to check the entrance behind me. A tall, blond-haired, woman was getting out of the car. She pushed the heavy glass door, stepped into the restaurant and into my life. A child who had looked for me her entire life was within touching distance.

Tears streamed down my face. Cupping my hands on her cheeks I looked at the image of my younger self. I hugged my baby girl for the first time in twenty-nine years. It was hard to let go.

I wiped tears from my eyes but there was no erasing my smile. We made small talk while we waited for the waitress.

The waitress stepped away from the table to get our order. The silence was awkward.

"I need to ask you one thing first."

"Ok"

Our eyes locked and without blinking Grace asked,

"Why did you give me up?"

That dreaded question was the first one she asked.

My answer tumbled out of my mouth like dice from a cup landing on the table with no order.

"I didn't have a job, or any way to take care of you. I thought we would end up living under a bridge or who knows where. My mom told me I couldn't come home, and I had nowhere to go."

"I wish you would have tried."

Her words stung and shame turned my gaze from her to the table. I made no response but, secretly wished I *had* tried.

Chapter 28

"Birthday celebrations were big in our house. Every year, on my birthday mom told the story of how God brought me into their lives. The only child they never thought they would have."

'Aunt Ellie was our greatest advocate. I told her that two years of trying to adopt and being rejected at every turn was too much. I would have to accept that we would never have a child. Your aunt Ellie encouraged me and promised to help. Members at the same church, one Sunday she asked Dean Thomas if he knew of any girls who might be considering giving a baby up for adoption. He had not. Then a miracle. Two weeks later Dean Thomas asked Ellie why she had inquired about someone giving a baby up for adoption. She explained that her sister and brother-in-law wanted to adopt.'

"Every time some new detail comes to light in this story, I see the hand of God and His timing."

"At age eleven, I started trying to find out who my biological parents were. Once a year I would call Mrs. "H" to convince her to give me any information on my birth mom, each time she kindly told me you requested your identity remain a secret.'

Time, tenacity and persistence must have softened her resolve. Each day, I ran to the mailbox looking for the letter. The day it came I tore open the envelope while I stood in front of the open mailbox near the street. A photo of two young children fell onto the grass as I sild the letter out of the envelope. It was a picture of Matthew and Deborah.

Mrs. "H" decided it would be okay to send pictures of your kids since it would not give away your identity. That picture was how I ultimately found you."

Using your maiden name to search Facebook and goggle returned no results. Name side up the picture Mrs. "H" had sent of your two kids, turned up on afternoon. I had been spelling it wrong. The correct spelling brought up a page for Matthew. He was friends with "Christine" and "Zoey." Seconds later I was looking at a photo of Matthew's mom."

"I have another question for you,

How did you know Mrs. "H" would have information about me?"

"My grandmother, Hannah, and she are best friends. They have known each other for 50 years. Ilene and Grandma Hannah were there when the adoption papers were signed."

"According to "Christine," she and your mom are good friends, right?"

"Yes, which is super cool. She is also Facebook friends with your son. I hoped she knew you."

"Did Christine know that you were adopted?"

"I don't know. We didn't really know each other well., My mom may have told her, but I knew she would tell me about you if I asked. In a text I asked her how she knew you and your son. She explained that you and she had met in Italy, become good friends and that your kids went to school together.

Do you remember the letter you wrote to me before I was born?"

"Yes, I do. Why?"

"I showed the letter to Christine. She recognized your handwriting and realized that I could be the baby you had giving up for adoption. In that letter you said you looked forward to seeing me in heaven. Did you want to meet me?"

"I understood that was not a possibility. So glad I was wrong."

"I am still trying to wrap my head around all of these connections. People, places and chance meetings which turned out to be less chance and more divinely planned. God is writing an amazing story, one of us should write it down one day."

"Like a Tapestry, with hundreds of threads each put in just the right place to make a beautiful finished product."

Chapter 29

Back home, I locked my car and rode the elevator to the eleventh floor. Floating on an air of unbelief as I walked down the hallway to our unit. Pleased to have met her and her husband. Thrilled to have spent the afternoon with the daughter I never knew, a heavy burden of guilt weighed heavy on my heart. I felt the pull of opposites trying to co-exist.

Nothing can prepare you for the real-life situation of meeting a previously unknown biological family member for the first time. The four of us sat in silence waiting for our server. Anxious glances, quick smiles, and far away looks. Grace and I had spoken for nearly four hours earlier in the day, our husbands were still strangers.

Dinner arrived and the food tasted especially delicious. Comfortable, if we had food on our plates. The dishes had been cleared; the awkward silence remained.

"So, Peter how do you feel about meeting Grace's biological mom?"

His reply created some needed comic relief.

"I'm good; this kind of thing happens to me all the time!"

Chapter 30

First coffee. The next morning, we met at a local shop inside an indoor mall and ordered lattes. The mall was home to several other shops. Artwork of local artists were featured on the walls throughout the space. A great place to start the day. We strolled and talked, the connection between mother and daughter felt oddly comfortable.

Shops situated along Cherry Creek were home to antiques, boutiques and record stores. The time flew by. Random and unexpected questions were her way to get to know me.

"How was it living with people you didn't know when you were pregnant with me?"

"It was peaceful. Living with the Patterson's was a blessing. I felt safe. They were kind and accommodating hosts. Despite their constant efforts to include me, I felt like an outsider. God continually shows me this is what loving each other looks like."

Letters, e-mails and phone calls helped strengthen the bond we established. A burgundy, hexagonal shaped box covered with brocade fabric came in the mail and inside were a pair of earrings Grace had made. A treasure box from a child thought lost forever.

Chapter 31

T hree months after my first volunteer shift at a Crisis Pregnancy Center, I requested to learn each position. One year later, I worked four to six shifts weekly and spoke at local churches on behalf of the Pregnancy Center. My weeks and my heart were full. Personal understanding of what these girls were going through allowed me to show compassion rooted in experience. Chances to speak candidly about abortion and the heartache associated with that decision was healing for me.

An e-mail from Grace asked if Antonio and I could come to Georgia and celebrate with her for her thirtieth birthday. My response was an emphatic yes; we were making plans. The day after receiving her e-mail I purchased the plane tickets.

Early February 2012 I answered the phone. It was Sarah. Preschool teacher, mid-wife, still married to her high school sweetheart and one of the "angels" God provided thirty years earlier to walk with me through a difficult time. She is the one person who saw my newborn baby before I did.

"I am so glad you called"

"I was so happy to read in your note that Grace found you and the two of you had the chance to meet. How was that?"

"It was exciting yet, at the same time, it caused a lot of anxiety. I was unsure how the reunion might play out, but it was a wonderful and blessed time."

"Your letter stated you volunteer at a Crisis Pregnancy Clinic, is that still the case?"

"Yes, it has been such a blessing, meeting and befriending the girls that come in. We offer parenting classes and free ultrasounds. I also attend local churches to speak about the Clinic and our ministry."

Sharing with her the circumstances and relationships which, over the years, had helped create this wonderful reunion story, her response was unexpected.

"I currently volunteer on the Board of Directors for a local Crisis Pregnancy Center here in Georgia. Each year we do a fundraiser and your story is so compelling. All the interconnected relationships and how Grace found you. It would be great if you could share this at our Annual Fundraising event coming up in April!"

"Wow, I have never spoken at a fundraiser before."

"I will need to present the recommendation to the board and get approval."

"In the meantime, can you send me information about the Clinic and contact information for the Director. I will need to speak with them before I can extend a formal invitation to speak."

Sarah would let me know once the board discussed it and voted. Still unsure what day in April the event would take place as soon as she had more details, she would call me. It had been two weeks since Sarah and I last spoke. After a conversation with the Director of the Clinic here in Vancouver, an official invitation to speak at the Fundraiser in Kansas had been extended. I eagerly accepted. Logistical arrangements were still being worked out, so the date had not been finalized.

Sarah knew Antonio and I were coming for Grace's birthday. I hoped the Fundraiser would not conflict with our visit. Waiting patiently, is not one of my glowing personality traits. It seemed to be taking far too long for Sarah to call me with information about the date of the Fundraiser. I decided to call and see if there was any word. I was only able to leave a message.

"Hello?"

"Hey, it's Sarah returning your call."

"I was wondering if the Board had decided on the date for the Fundraiser and if I was still on to speak?"

"Yes, you are still on to speak and we decided on the fourteenth."

My heart sank; that was Grace's birthday. Then my eyes widened as a smile formed. Possibly I could speak at the fundraiser and see Grace. They were both in Georgia.

"Ok. That is Grace's birthday. We are planning to spend it with her there in Georgia."

Wondering if she had made big plans or if she would consider spending the evening of her 30th at a fundraiser, my mind was swirling with thoughts. Remembering the letter Evelyn had written and sensing her genuine concern for me, I daringly suggested that maybe, if Grace agreed to attend the fundraiser that possibly her mom and dad would agree to attend as well.

"That would be so amazing! Do you think Grace would want to do that on her birthday?"

"I don't know but I will ask the next time I talk to her."

Sarah continued, "I didn't say anything before because I was waiting for a response but, Pastor Howard will be there, and I just got confirmation today that the Patterson's are also planning to be there."

Chapter 32

The hotel, close to the airport, was miles from the kids' house. The plane arrived at 11 pm. The next day we would drive to Grace and Peter's' place.

"I really hate this hotel" I snapped. "I knew we should have gone somewhere different! I can't believe how far we need to drive to get there. Did you see how small the bathroom is?"

The day before, Deborah, her husband and two young boys arrived from Europe. It would be the first time that both of my daughters and me would be together. Plus, being Nana to my grandsons was one of the most joyous "occupations" of all time. Why was I so irritable and anxious? I apologized to my husband for complaining and being grumpy. In his loving and supportive way, he encouraged me to just breathe and assured me everything would be okay. Then he made me laugh by saying

"It could be worse it could be a community bathroom."

He was right; things can always be worse. I rolled my eyes and chuckled.

The drive wasn't bad, and we got to enjoy the countryside. It gave me time to think about all that was to happen; meeting the people who had raised my daughter, speaking at a fundraiser – a first for me, and seeing people who knew me at my most vulnerable and needy. As we neared the house I started to panic, then tears welled up in my eyes.

"We have arrived."

I just looked at my husband. The look on my face caused him to reach over and grab my hand and say,

"Everything's going to be ok."

Deborah and Grace were walking arm in arm down the steps of the front porch as I unbuckled my seatbelt and slowly got out of the car. Immediately I noticed they were wearing matching jackets! I quickly walked toward them and hugged them both. I wished my arms were longer so I could have hugged them harder. Tears streamed down my face when my Antonio said,

"Turn around so I can get a photo of the three of you."

I smoothed the wetness from my face and with one daughter on either side, he snapped a picture.

Chapter 33

The letter from Evelyn was graciously written. She was looking forward to meeting me. Like the feelings of trepidation about meeting Grace, I was a nervous mess considering meeting the couple who had raised her and taught her to love the Lord. I was humbled by knowing that she and her husband lived their faith and ministered to others. This knowledge shined a spotlight on my shame.

I tried to put myself in her shoes and consider how I would feel meeting the birth mom of my child. It was impossible for me to see outside of myself. I was just as grateful for them as she had said she was for me.

"Wake up honey; we have to get ready to meet the kids at the café."

While getting ready I rehearsed saying hello to her.

'Hello Evelyn. Hi there Evelyn. Hi, it is nice to meet you.'

Nothing sounded right. I would strike up conversations with strangers and welcomed the chance to emcee or to speak. I had done presentations to hundreds of military families and counseled young women in crisis. I earned a Master's Degree in Business, yet meeting my baby's adoptive parents made my knees buckle.

Vulnerable and exposed, two emotions I knew well. Staring my old nemesis' in the face was unacceptable. I told myself it did not matter what she thought of me. My fear was unfounded, I prayed for the Lord to give me strength.

Antonio held the car door for me. Once our seatbelts were fastened, we rode in relative silence for most of the drive. He parked directly across the street from the café. As he put the car into park, I blurted out; "I can't do it. I don't want to meet them."

There was no response from him until he turned off the engine.

"Come on, get out, the café is right there across the street. You will be fine."

Frozen in the seat, my belt still buckled. My loving husband opened the passenger side door, reached across my waist and unbuckled my seatbelt. He smiled and put out his hand to help me out of the car.

"I will walk you across the street then I will be back later for lunch."

Standing outside of the door of the café situated in a quaint downtown area of an Atlanta suburb, I watched my husband walk back across the street, get into the rental car then drive away.

A bell, attached to door, rang as I slowly opened it. The ringing caused everyone in the small café to look toward the door. Smiling sheepishly, I glanced around the room. I had no way of knowing which of the women in the café she might be.

It was apparent she knew what I looked like and was there because I heard someone call out my name.

"Mary!"

Evelyn motioned me over to the small table where she was sitting. She stood up and gave me the biggest hug. I must have looked ridiculous, my arms to my side being bear hugged by this woman I had never met. Her positive and kind gesture blindsided me.

I squeaked out a low volume, "Hi?!"

Her smile never wavered, as she invited me to sit down.

"This place is a favorite of mine. I come here every week. My parents live close by."

She recommended the coffee and pastries. Evelyn also made sure that I knew they offered vegan and Gluten Free options. Coffee was a good idea. Thankful for a few minutes to settle into my new surroundings and take some deep breaths to slow down my heart rate.

"Mary, I want you to know that Larry and I have always thought of you as being courageous and selfless. You gave us the chance to be parents and for that we are eternally grateful. However, we are also aware of the pain this must have caused you. We told Grace about you each year on her birthday and prayed for you."

"Why would you do that?".

She took my hand and cradled it in both of hers,

"We knew you gave her up because it was the best thing for the baby but the hardest thing for you."

Evelyn reiterated what she had written in her letter. How she ached to have children but was unable to conceive.

"I had been in the hospital for months with no clear diagnosis until one morning while on rounds my doctor told me it was a treatable condition. I breathed a sigh of relief as the doctor continued.

'However, one of the side effects of this particular condition is that you will not be able to have children of your own.'

The news hit me hard. Larry and I talked about how we wanted to have a large family. I knew what I had to do when he next visited. Tearfully I told him what the doctor said about not being able to conceive. I tried to call off the engagement. He would not hear of it. He loved me and wanted to marry me. We were married in 1978. We checked into adoption as soon as we got back from our honeymoon. My health issues were always a roadblock and we received rejection letters from nearly every agency we applied to. It seemed that we would have a childless future.

Ellie and I have always been close, and she called often to check in and encourage me. That day I was feeling pretty good despite that fact that we got another rejection letter from the last adoption agency. I told my sister I was not sure how many more rejections we could take. We had been trying for over two years. I was resigned to the fact that we would never have a child."

"That must have been so hard for you and Larry."

"It was not what we wanted for our lives, but we trusted God to direct our path. Ellie was and still is very tenacious. She was adamant that the adoption agencies were wrong and that we would be great parents. She vowed to do whatever she could to help make that happen."

"Ellie was ecstatic when two weeks later Dean Thomas approached her and explained that he knew of a young woman who needed a couple to adopt her baby. This had never happened to him in all his time in leadership at the College."

I responded,

"Another example of God's timing."

"Mary, I have some gifts for you that I would like you to open before our husbands and kids arrive. My brows curled into an inquisitive look.

She first handed me a small gift bag. The weight of the package was more than one would imagine from its size. I thanked her as I began to unwrap it.

Approximately six inches by six inches, a fabric cover with flowers which had been created with small shiny gold and cooper colored sequins and embroidered leaves stitched with gold thread. An opening, four inches by two inches, on the front of the album displayed a picture of a baby sitting on someone's lap.

"The baby is Grace just after we brought her home. I am the one holding her."

I touched the picture as if I could touch my baby. Picture after picture of my little girl as she grew. Pictures of family and of Evelyn and Larry. Seeing pictures of this child was like seeing myself reincarnated. The last photo was of Grace giving Evelyn, a kiss. The glasses she wore, the color of her hair and the left side profile; the picture could have been of me at that age.

The second package was nearly the size of the table. Removing the plain brown paper revealed a child's drawing with a quote. The drawing, a scene from a storybook. Grace had drawn the picture and hand-written the quote from *'The Velveteen Rabbit.'* "Grace gave this to me for Mother's Day one year. This was my favorite story as a child and she knew this was my favorite part of the book." Evelyn wanted me to have this copy.

My tear-filled eyes overflowed. This mother was sharing a part of Grace's childhood with these small gestures. Evelyn's kindness and acceptance in allowing me to be a part of both she and Grace's life were a display of selflessness.

A line from the first note Evelyn sent to me just weeks earlier came to mind, "There is no greater song that that of the redeemed. So glad we are all part of history." This woman, a stranger, gave me something I never thought possible; unconditional love. She cared for a life that was precious to me. The loving arms of God reached to me from one of the redeemed.

Searching through my purse for a tissue, the bell on the door of the café rang. It was Antonio. With tears trickling down my cheeks I walked towards him and hugged him.

"Are you ok?"

I took his hand and led him to the table where Evelyn sat and introduced her.

Seconds later, the door opened again. Grace, her husband Peter, Deborah, her husband and my two grandsons all converged on the cafe at once. A few minutes later my dear friend Christine and her daughter Zoey arrived. Larry had quietly slipped in while the waitress was moving tables and chairs. Introductions were made and we sat down to have a meal together.

Chapter 34

That evening, a celebratory party at Grace and Peter's house. The guest list included my college roommate Amanda and her husband. On the drive back to the hotel, my husband, chauffeur, and best friend, let me alone with my thoughts. No doubt he was tired and ready for some rest as well. We would try to sleep in the next day before driving to the Georgia town where the fundraiser would be held. Once there we would check into the local hotel which was being paid for by the Pregnancy Center. The drive was not familiar. It had been thirty years since I had been there. The town was not recognizable to me either.

Settling into our room, the plan was to nap since I would be speaking that evening. However, spending time with my grandsons was a rare opportunity. Napping could wait.

We left the hotel later than planned. The love and compassion shown to me decades before was a gift I could never repay. My life to that point had been an exercise to repay these and others who had picked me up, placed me back on my feet, and pointed me in the right direction. Sobriety, an education and life as a Christian woman. It was important they knew their kindness, efforts and resources had not been wasted. Once I saw the faces of these amazing people, and felt the love in their hugs, all fear and doubts subsided.

Tables filled the back room of a local church, a large kitchen close by. A crowd of 100 would hear my story. A story of Grace, reunion and renewal to bring in needed donations to the Crisis Pregnancy Center in a small Georgia town where Grace was born.

"God has created a beautiful story marked with His fingerprints. I have the privilege of sharing this story with you tonight. The people, places and events which took place over the past eighty years, show this is a story only God could have written. Sarah, who gave that beautiful introduction was there when my baby was born, coached me prior to the birth, and helped alleviate fear of giving birth for the first time. The Patterson family graciously opened their home to me. Pastor Howard, the congregation, and other "angels" who gave of their time, resources and unconditional love to help me and my unborn child are here this evening. I am truly thankful for each of you. I would not be the person I am had it not been for your selflessness and love.

If we allow him to, God weaves the circumstances of our lives into a something beautiful and useful. Psalm 117:2 says 'His great love towards us and the faithfulness of the Lord endures forever, praise the Lord.'

My faith is stronger today than yesterday. My own failures as much as others have taught me to trust. Life as a child was difficult. Hypocrisy, hatred and abuse characterized eighteen years of my life. I believed the best way to feel loved was through sexual contact. However, my actions made me feel worse. On two separate occasions I chose to have abortions. Broken promises and commandments did not result in love.

The news of another pregnancy came three months after my second abortion. I failed to resist temptation at the cost of another innocent life. Where was the love I needed and who would give it to me? The most unlikely place. Bible college.

Christ followers reached out in love and mercy based on the word of a twenty-year-old, pregnant, unmarried student who professed belief in Jesus. There had to be a catch. There was.

Move into the home of wonderful people and attend church where God's word is preached. Work at a job provided for you. Attend counseling sessions and Lamaze classes, free of charge. Lastly, the unborn child will be cared for through adoption to a Christian couple.

Thirty years later I stand here humbled by your love."

The crowd watched as a birthday cake was wheeled out.

"Thirty years ago, in this town, a baby girl was born. Her parents named her Grace and she is here tonight."

Surprised, Grace thanked me and blew out the candles to the delight of the audience. I will never forget, sharing her thirtieth birthday with her and her parents, her half-sister and the Christian people who sacrificially gave us lifesaving gifts!

Chapter 35

Grace and Peter moved to Colorado, the same year our youngest brother was turning fifty. My sister and I planned a surprise trip to Florida where he lived. A lineage where adults live three to four decades, this is a celebratory milestone.

I wanted to give him a meaningful and significant gift. I made him a scrapbook. Focusing on his life, but also remembering those family members who had come before.

Putting together the pieces of our lives was not too difficult. Twenty years earlier Ruth, our mother, died from complications of Breast Cancer. Sifting through journals and writings we found after mom died, I came across several letters I had never seen before.

Handwritten on lined yellow paper about five inches by four inches it floated to the carpet from the ratty and falling apart folder it had been housed in for over forty years, these five pages would reveal a lifetime of pain.

Reading the words in Charles' handwriting made me cringe, cry, and feel intense sadness. Some of what he had gone through was horrific. Understanding that he had no role model for parenthood and all that he saw growing up was rage and hate and death, my feelings and perspective changed slightly. Not excusing his behavior, there was a twinge of sympathy.

Chapter 36

The crisp cool air of spring trying to let go of the cold winter air, and the way the sun danced on the water reminded me of the day I met Grace. Once the door opened, I made my way towards the table where she sat. This woman had left an inerasable mark on my heart

Eighteen months earlier her husband was killed in a car accident. Her decision to move to a place closer to her family was welcome news and a chance to reconnect. Christine looked out the window. I touched her on the shoulder. A smile emerged and her curly brown hair, streaked with gray, seemed to shake as if it were greeting me.

"It is so good to see you again."

"I am so excited you are here."

"After my husband died, I prayed for a job. The move was intentional. I relocated because I accepted a position at a local non-profit and start in two weeks."

"That is awesome. I am so happy for you. Which non-profit is it?"

"The same one that you volunteer for. The pregnancy center on Main Street."

"What? That is so cool. How great you found a job and for us to work together. Don't worry, I am able to be friends and recognize your authority at work."

One Year Later

One early fall afternoon, the phone rang at the clinic and the caller asked to speak to Christine.

I just finished my shift at the Pregnancy Clinic that afternoon. Christine met me in the hall as I put on my coat.

"Do you have a minute to talk before you leave?"

"Sure."

Once in her office I sat down in the overstuffed chair situated in a corner. The table to the left of the chair was home to a stuffed dragon.

"The phone call was from a Bible College here in Denver. A young student just discovered she is six weeks pregnant, and Dean Morris wondered if we could help"

Christine and I looked at each other smiled then nodded our heads in syncopated agreement, we knew we would do all we could to help this young lady.

Conclusion

An emotional journey of epic proportions. Anger, tears, regret. Also hope, forgiveness, and peace. I see blessing in situations and circumstances I once considered punishment.

Psalm 119:17 says

"I know O LORD that your judgments are fair and that in faithfulness you have disciplined me."

Amplified Bible

A life that trusts more and honors God is my prayer for the next chapters of my life.

The years after Grace and Peter moved to Colorado we visited often, shared holidays and began a journey I hoped would last longer. It was hard for her to continue the journey so in her last email she asked that for the future we suspend our relationship. I struggled to understand her reaction, but found it is common in adults who have reconnected with their biological parents to become overwhelmed and need to step away from the relationship.

I wonder how different our lives would have been if I had kept her. I would not have to bear the pain of giving her up a second time. I am thankful for the years I was able to be a part of her life, but I miss her.

The author of this story would have ended with the credits "And they lived happily ever after …" However, God is the author and, the ending is still very much unknown.

CPSIA information can be obtained
at www.ICGtesting.com
Printed in the USA
LVHW081304070222
710466LV00020B/261